BREAKIN' IN

REAL ESTATE RESCUE COZY MYSTERIES, BOOK
6

PATTI BENNING

SUMMER PRESCOTT BOOKS PUBLISHING

CHAPTER ONE

A rumble of thunder made the old windowpanes in Flora Abner's living room shake. She turned so she could look out the window behind the couch she was sitting on in time to see the dark, cloudy sky outside light up with a lightning strike. The white rocks of her driveway were slick with rain, and the branches of the trees across the road were waving in the wind.

It was the perfect night for staying in and eating dinner in front of her TV.

The oven beeped, signaling to Flora that her frozen pizza was done cooking. She paused to run her hand along her cat's back, combing her fingers through the Persian's fluffy white fur.

"Don't worry, Amaretto. It's just a storm. It won't hurt you."

Her cat had never been a fan of thunderstorms, but it seemed to have gotten worse since they moved to Kentucky. The storms seemed much closer here, in her old country farmhouse, than they had in the middle of Chicago.

The cat watched, unblinking, as Flora stood up and went into the kitchen, snatching her cell phone off of the coffee table on the way. She cracked the oven open to eye her chicken and artichoke pizza, and determined it needed another couple of minutes, so she took a seat at the kitchen table, her eyes finding the window above the sink.

Despite her words to Amaretto, it *was* a bad storm. The trees lining her property were bending and swaying, and she was certain she would find a lot of broken limbs and branches in her yard come tomorrow. She was glad that she and Grady had finished repairing the small storage shed behind the house a few weeks ago, because if they hadn't, this storm may have been its death-knell.

Having a leak-free roof was a relief too. She would never forget the stress of watching water drip down from the upstairs ceiling whenever it rained, like it had early this spring when she first moved to Warbler. The house really had come a long way since she bought it, though it still had a long way to go before she could sell it for the profit she needed to both pay her aunt back the loan that had let Flora get this new start on her life, and to purchase her next project house.

Another rumble of thunder made Flora feel like her bones were vibrating, and the lights in the kitchen flickered. She held her breath, but they stayed on. It was one thing to curl up on the couch with some pizza and a movie while the storm raged outside — it would be another matter entirely if she was stuck here all night with no power.

She got up to check the pizza again and saw the golden-brown color of the cheese along the crust that told her it was done. She took it out with a pair of oven mitts and set it on the stove to cool while she turned off the oven and set a large cutting board and a pizza cutter on the counter.

Her phone started ringing, a cheerful, bright sound that made her jump. It was nearly nine on a weekday night, and almost everyone she knew would text before they called unless it was urgent, which meant either it was a family emergency, or the call was from Grady — the one person she knew who didn't have a cell phone and instead made do with only a landline phone.

She smiled when she picked up her phone and

saw his name on the screen. After answering the call, she set it on speaker and put the phone on the counter while she got a plate and a glass out of the cupboard.

"Hey," she said. "Crazy storm, huh?"

"Yeah, it's gonna be a bad one," Grady's familiar voice said. "You doin' all right? The shed's holding up?"

She paused in folding a napkin. "Why? Do you think it *won't* hold up? Oh my goodness, was all of our work for nothing?"

He chuckled. "It should be fine. I'm just checking in."

She glanced out the window above the sink again. From this angle, she could see the shed. "It looks like it's doing fine." She hesitated. "I feel a little bad about kicking that raccoon out now, though. All of the wild animals have to be miserable tonight."

"The raccoon will be fine," he told her, sounding amused. "Let me know if you need anything, all right? The power might go out, and some of the trees you've got on your land look like they might not hold up so well."

Flora grinned as she started cutting the pizza. "Aww. You're worried about me."

He scoffed, and she knew him well enough to tell

4

he was embarrassed. "Just making sure you'll be okay, since you're a city girl and all."

"I appreciate it, Grady," she said sincerely. "I'd invite you over to join me for pizza and a movie, but…" She looked outside again as wind drove the rain against the kitchen window. "Something tells me it isn't safe to drive."

"I knew someone who was killed by a tree limb falling on his car while he was driving during a storm like this," Grady said. Flora shuddered.

"Yeah, definitely not safe. If I lose power or something, I'll give you a call, though. My phone is almost fully charged, so it should be fine until morning. You stay safe too."

"I will," he promised. "See ya, Flora."

She said her goodbyes and ended the call before piling a few slices of pizza on her plate. After filling her glass with water, she tucked her phone into her back packet and carried her plate and glass back into the living room, where Amaretto was still huddled on the couch.

"I hate that you look so scared," Flora told the cat as she sat down. "Do you want a piece of chicken? Look, it's still warm. Fresh out of the oven. It's even got a little bit of cheese on it."

She plucked a piece of chicken off the pizza, and as she tried to tempt her frightened cat into eating it, she thought about Grady. Their relationship was changing… slowly. They had gone out on one date so far, and both of them had been a little awkward during it, but after hugging her goodbye at the end of it, Grady had asked her out on another one and she had agreed, though they hadn't arranged anything yet.

A side effect was that all of their other interactions since had held that same edge of awkwardness and uncertainty. Flora hoped it would go away soon, because she missed how easy things had been between the two of them before.

A clap of thunder and flash of lightning happened at almost the same instant, and Amaretto bolted from where she had been sniffing the piece of chicken in Flora's hand. The cat vanished into Flora's bedroom, the small room right off the living room that she had never quite moved away from sleeping in, and presumably hid under her bed. Flora sat back with a sigh, leaving the piece of chicken on her napkin while she took her first bite of pizza. She didn't know how to help Amaretto, and decided to let the cat hide for now. With luck, the storm would pass them over quickly.

As she chewed her pizza, which was actually pretty good considering that it was one of the cheaper frozen ones, she hit play on the TV remote and the movie she was watching started back up. It was an old slasher flick, which was perfect for a night like this. Pizza, a horror movie, a storm raging outside... sure, she might have to resort to asking her neighbor, Natalie, to give her the numbers of the two young men who did her yard work to help her clean up her yard when it was over, but it made for the perfect cozy evening at home.

A clap of thunder so loud it rattled her plate made her jump, and the room illuminated with a flash of lightning that followed right on its tail. The TV shut off without her touching the remote, and the house fell silent and dark. Slowly, Flora reached for the lamp on the side table beside the couch, but when she toggled the switch, it remained dark.

"Shoot," she muttered. She waited for a few seconds, but the power didn't miraculously return. Sighing, she shoved the rest of her first slice of pizza into her mouth and got up to find the flashlight that she kept just inside the basement door.

Ignoring the way the dark basement stairs seemed to stretch infinitely downwards, she snagged the flashlight and shut the basement door firmly before switching it on. Wind howled through the cracks and crevasses of the old house as Flora returned to the living room, the beam of light guiding her way.

"Spooky," she murmured as the wind gusted and gave an extra loud moan.

The sound of shattering glass came from over her head and she let out a yelp, nearly dropping the flashlight in her surprise. It must have been an upstairs window breaking — that was the only thing she could think of that might break up there, besides the bathroom mirror and the lamp on the bedside table in the newly renovated guest room.

She hurried upstairs, the flashlight's beam bumping and bobbing as she ran. She checked the empty room first, but it was just as it had been the last time she peeked inside. With a feeling of dread, she hurried into the guest room and stopped short.

The gusting wind had blown a broken branch right into the window. Broken glass and a torrent of rain poured across the wooden floors she had just recently refinished and shards of glass sparkled on the bedspread of the brand-new bed that had arrived only a week ago. The branch lay half through the window, and a new gust of wind sent one of the wet leaves across the room to splat right on Flora's face.

She stared at the mess in shock. Forget the movie downstairs — this was the most horrifying thing she had seen all night.

CHAPTER TWO

Flora glowered at the broken glass and water that covered the floor in the guest bedroom, her arms crossed over her chest. It was morning now, and the storm had broken hours ago. A tarp rustled in the breeze in place of the broken glass. She had attached it — sloppily — to the window frame the night before in an effort to keep the water damage to a minimum, but she wasn't sure if it had done much good. The room was a *mess*.

To make matters worse, it wasn't the only place in the house water had gotten in. When she woke up an hour ago, her first surprise had been a pleasant one — the power was back on. It went downhill after that when she discovered that the security camera at her front door must have been fried when the power surged, because it wasn't working. Then, while she was filling the coffee pot with water for her morning caffeine, she noticed water on the kitchen windowsill.

That led to a discovery that roughly a third of the windows in her house were leaking at least some amount of water, and since all of the house's windows were older than she was, she knew it was only a matter of time until the rest of them started leaking too.

She was going to have to bite the bullet and get the windows replaced. Professionally. There was a lot that she was willing to do herself, but replacing every window in the house was a little bit above her skill level, and even with Grady's help, it would take them a long time. Too long, when it was starting to get chillier outside and her aunt was going to be coming to stay for Thanksgiving in just a couple of months.

Sighing, Flora started pushing the shards of glass into a pile with a mop. She got the room cleaned up enough that neither she nor Amaretto would cut their feet accidentally if they came in here, then stepped out into the hallway, shutting the door firmly behind her. The last thing she needed was for her cat to escape through the broken window on top of every-thing else.

After that, she decided to kill two birds with one

stone and go over to visit her elderly neighbors, Beth and Tim York. She wanted to check on them after the storm, but she also wanted a recommendation for which company to hire to replace her windows, and who better to ask than a woman who has lived in Warbler her entire life?

She checked on Amaretto, who was happily licking her bowl clean in the kitchen. The cat's fear from the night before seemed to have vanished with the morning sun.

"Once I get this sorted out, we'll try the harness again," Flora promised. She had been trying to harness train the cat so she could go outside, and it was going about as well as she could hope. Amaretto let her put the harness on without complaint now, but as soon as there was any tension on the leash, the cat went boneless and refused to move until Flora took it off.

They would get there, one day. She was sure of it.

She put her shoes on, grabbed her purse, and slipped her phone into her back pocket, then stepped outside. She debated on whether to take her truck over to Beth's or walk there, but the dirt road was a muddy mess, so she decided to drive.

By the time Flora parked in her neighbor's driveway — the term was used generously, since Beth lived nearly a quarter of a mile down the road — the older woman was standing on her front porch and waving cheerily in greeting.

Flora waved back as she got out of the truck. "Did you see me driving over?" she asked as she approached the front porch.

"I thought you might be Nolan," Beth replied. "But I'm glad to see you too! How did you fare in the storm last night? It was a bad one."

Flora had no idea who Nolan was, but Beth's question reminded her of one of her reasons for coming over, so she let her curiosity go and said, "Well, we survived, but one of the upstairs windows didn't. The storm sent a branch right through it, and I found out that some of my other windows have started leaking. I think I need to replace them all — half of them don't even match, and they're all old. Do you know of any good window companies in the area?"

"I'll give you the number for the company who did our windows a few years ago," Beth said. She waved Flora closer. "Come on in, dear. I'll need a few minutes to find the number. You can look at our windows while I'm at it, to see what you think of the work. We were very pleased, I can tell you that. Leave the door open, will you? I need to keep an ear out for Nolan. Sammy's on his cable out back, so you don't have to worry about him getting out."

Flora worked through the deluge of information as she followed Beth into the house, leaving the door open behind her as instructed. Sammy was Beth's droopy Basset hound, and one of the laziest dogs Flora had ever met. It was hard to imagine him having the energy to actually run away if the opportunity presented itself, but she supposed he could be full of surprises.

"Who's Nolan?" Flora asked as she trailed Beth into the kitchen. "I don't think I've met him."

"Oh, I haven't told you? The grocery store started offering a grocery delivery service a couple of weeks ago. Senior citizens only have to pay a tip on top of the price of the goods. It's such a wonderful innovation. I don't have to wait until the bus comes on the weekends to go shopping now. Nolan is the young man who delivers out here. He's such a sweetheart. You should meet him — he's never mentioned a girlfriend." Beth winked at her, and Flora wrinkled her nose.

"No matchmaking, please," she said as Beth started rifling through her address book. "Changing the topic — how did you two hold up during the storm? Do you need any help picking up branches?"

"Oh, we managed well enough. You're such a kind girl, but I think I'll have those two boys who have been doing yard work for Natalie help me out. I'm sure they could use the money, and I know you're going to be busy with your own yard. Speaking of, would you mind stopping by her house before you go home? I made a lovely flower arrangement for her, to brighten her place up. I'd take it over myself, but with the roads like they are, I'm worried I'd slip and fall."

"Sure, I can drop it off," Flora said. Natalie wasn't a fan of hers, but they could be civil when they had to be.

"Thanks, dear. Ah, here's the number. Let me just copy it over for you…"

Beth wrote the number down on an index card and handed it over to Flora, who thanked her as she took it. The sound of tires on gravel caught their attention.

"That must be Nolan. Here, I'll get those flowers for you."

Beth hurried into the living room and handed Flora a vase with an arrangement of the last of the summer's flowers in it just as someone knocked on the frame of the open door. A man a few years younger than Flora poked his head into the house.

"Ms. York? I have your delivery."

"Nolan, I'm glad you made it. I'll help you bring

the bags in," Beth said. Flora slipped out the door past him with a polite nod, hoping to get away before the older woman remembered her matchmaking dreams. She put the flowers on the floor of the passenger side of the truck carefully, then walked around to the driver's side, pausing to wave goodbye to Beth. Nolan had parked his van beside the truck, giving her space to get out. He came around the back of the van, his arms loaded down with bags of groceries, as they were saying goodbye.

"Good luck with your windows, dear," Beth called out. "I hope the repairs don't take too long."

"Thanks," Flora called back. "And thanks for the number! I'll get these flowers to Natalie, and I'll see you later."

She waved one final time after getting into her truck, then backed out of the driveway. She would have to call the window company after giving the flowers to Natalie, and she had a feeling she was going to have to reschedule her lunch with Linus, another newcomer to town she had gotten friendly with a while ago. This day was turning out to be a lot busier than she had expected.

CHAPTER THREE

Natalie's yard hadn't fared as well as Flora's or Beth's had. While Flora's house was in the center of a large, grassy yard that was bordered by trees, Natalie's was tucked right into the forest with only a small grassy area out front. When Flora turned into her driveway, the first thing she noticed was the pile of branches sitting by the road. The second thing she noticed was the two young men dragging even more branches from around the back of the house. There were even sticks and branches on the roof, though thankfully none large enough to damage the structure.

She parked her truck next to the van she assumed belonged to the workers, and behind the red sedan that Natalie owned. The last time she was here, she had witnessed Natalie's brother getting arrested, and she couldn't say she was thrilled to be back. She had hardly spoken to the other woman since that incident, though Beth chattered and gossiped enough Flora felt she had managed to keep up with her other neighbor pretty well anyway.

After grabbing the flowers from the passenger door footwell, Flora approached the house, pausing only to wave at one of the young men who was dragging a heavy tree limb towards the road. When Beth told her that Natalie had hired the pair to do her yard work for a very good price, she had been a little tempted to get their number herself, because she hated going around her yard to pick up sticks before mowing every time — all of that stooping and standing back up made her back hurt, though admitting to such a thing made her feel old. In the end, she had decided against it because she *was* trying to save money where she could, and the mowing season was almost over.

Maybe it would be worth it to hire them for one job now, though. She toyed with the thought as she walked up to the front porch, and decided that paying them for a couple of hours' worth of labor to pick up the broken branches and sticks from the storm would be worth it to save her back.

She held the vase in one hand as she knocked on

Natalie's front door with the other. It took a moment for the other woman to open it, and when she did, her expression morphed into a frown as soon as she saw who had knocked.

"Yes?" she said shortly.

"These are from Beth. She asked me to drop them off for her — she's busy with a grocery delivery right now, and didn't want to risk walking with the road so muddy."

"Thanks." Natalie took the flowers from Flora, her lips evening out into something a little more neutral. "Pardon the yard. Cleanup after that storm is taking a while."

"I think we're all feeling the after-effect of that storm," Flora replied, giving Natalie her best friendly smile. She understood why the other woman didn't want much to do with her, but she really would have liked to be on better terms with her. "The wind sent a branch right through one of my windows. I'm going to have to get it replaced, and hope it doesn't storm again in the meantime because I don't think the tarp I put up is quite going to cut it."

"Well, I'm sure you'll get it figured out," Natalie said, already stepping back and poised to shut the door. "Thank you for delivering the flowers for Beth. Have a nice day."

She shut the door in Flora's face. Sighing, she turned to go back to her truck, but changed course when she noticed one of the young men walking back towards the house from the pile of tree limbs. She waved to get his attention and he met her partway across the yard.

"Hi there," she said. "I'm Flora Abner, and I live just down the road. I was wondering if you're open to taking more work on?"

"I'm Tucker," he said, shaking her hand. He looked like he was college-age, with dark blonde hair and a deep tan that spoke of many hours spent outside over the summer. "And that's Duncan." He waved at his companion, who looked to be about the same age, though with darker hair and a paler complexion. "We're going to be pretty busy for the next couple of days, but if you're not in a hurry, we'd be happy to take whatever job you have for us."

She would probably only have to mow one more time this year, and not for another couple of weeks, so she decided she didn't mind waiting to get the sticks picked up. "That's fine. It'll be the same as this — I need the debris from the storm out of my yard. I'm the last house on this side of the road, you can't miss it."

"Let me get my phone and I'll get your number,"

Tucker said. "I'll give you our card too. We're always happy to find more clients."

Flora called the window company when she got home a few minutes later. The earliest they would be able to come out was Tuesday of next week, so she battened down the broken window and spent the weekend removing the wallpaper in the kitchen. Tucker and Duncan got back to her on Monday to tell her they could come work on her yard the next day, and she confirmed with the window company that they were coming out tomorrow too. Hopefully by Wednesday, all of the damage the storm had caused to both the house and the yard would be gone.

She woke up bright and early on Tuesday morning to get ready for the window repair people. The window replacement would likely take all day, and she didn't want to risk Amaretto getting out, so she arranged the cat's supplies in the basement and locked her down there with a handful of treats to make up for it.

"I'm sorry, sweetie," she said through the closed basement door. "It's going to be a long day, I know, but things will be back to normal tomorrow, I promise."

She scribbled out a sign warning the repair men not to open the basement door, then got started on painting the kitchen a cheerful yellow while she waited for the various workers to arrive.

The day was a busy one. The team that was replacing the windows arrived first, and she spent a good half hour talking to them. She was certain the man she had spoken to on the phone had told her they would be able to get the job finished in a day, but apparently she was wrong, because she learned it would take them at least two days to finish the work, assuming they didn't hit any delays. She wasn't thrilled at the thought of sleeping in a house with only half its windows installed, and knew she couldn't keep Amaretto in the basement for that long. She sent a text off to Violet, knowing her friend would provide a sympathetic ear to complain to, then hurried outside when she saw Tucker and Duncan pull up in their van so she could make sure they knew what parts of her yard to focus on.

It was strange to return to her painting with other people in the house, working on it and making noise. She was used to being here alone or with her friends. This was only the second time she had hired professionals to do something, and though she didn't regret deciding not to tackle the windows herself, she still felt a little guilty about it. She was spending a *lot* of money on this. She would just have to hope she would be able to sell the house for as much as she needed to, so she could pay her aunt back and continue her career of flipping houses.

She was in the middle of taping off the junction between the countertop and the wall when her phone chimed with an incoming text message. A glance at the screen showed her it was from Violet, so she put the roll of blue painter's tape down and picked up the phone.

Bummer, but they do have a lot of windows to replace. Two days isn't that bad. Do you want to spend the night here with Amaretto? I don't have a spare bedroom, but the couch is comfortable enough.

The offer was a kind one, and Flora only had to consider her options for a moment before she accepted it. A night spent in Violet's living room would be a lot more comfortable than one spent in a house with holes where the windows should be and an unhappy cat locked in the basement.

You are a lifesaver. We'll come over around 8, and I'll buy dinner as thanks. Just let me know what you want me to pick up!

She smiled. These next two days would be hectic, but it would all be worth it by the time the projects were done.

She picked up her phone again to send a quick

text message to Linus, a fellow newcomer to town who she was supposed to have lunch with tomorrow.

Sorry, but I think I'm going to have to reschedule. I'm going to be staying the night at a friend's while my windows are replaced, and I'm not sure how busy things will be in the morning. Could we meet Thursday instead?

He responded almost immediately to tell her Thursday was fine, and not to worry about it. She was glad her friends were so understanding. The storm damage might be annoying, but before long, it would be nothing but a faint memory, and she would have some nice new windows to show for it.

CHAPTER FOUR

Flora worked on the kitchen all day, until the window installers left around six. One wall in the kitchen was a cheerful yellow, and another wall was half finished. Tucker and Duncan were still working outside, dragging sticks and branches to the pile of wooden scraps she asked them to make just inside the tree line. Once the wood dried a little, it would be perfect for bonfires. She could hear music playing from a speaker one of them was carrying. They seemed to be almost done with the yard, but she wanted to get going to Violet's. Her friend was already out of work, but Violet had to wake up early the next morning, so if they wanted to kick back with some take-out and watch a movie, the sooner she got there, the better.

After packing Amaretto into her carrier and

putting the cat's necessary belongings into her truck, she ventured across the yard to speak to the men. Duncan was the one who spotted her approaching this time. He paused the music that was coming from a Bluetooth speaker on his belt and raised a hand in greeting.

"I'm about to head out," Flora told him. "Are you two okay to finish up this evening while I'm gone, or will you need to come back tomorrow? I probably won't be back until mid-morning, so I'd rather pay you now if that's possible."

"We'll be done here in about an hour," he told her. "Just got the back part left to do."

"Great." She smiled. "Thanks again for doing this. What do I owe you? I'll get you the cash before I go."

He told her, and she returned to the house to get the money. After paying them, she shoved a change of clothes and some pajamas into her overnight bag, grabbed her phone charger, and hefted Amaretto's carrier. The cat let out a forlorn sounding meow.

"I know, I know," Flora said, trying to keep her voice soothing. "It's been a crazy day, huh? Things will be back to normal soon, I promise."

She carried everything out to the front porch, where she had to put the cat's carrier down to free a hand so she could lock the door. She gave a quiet snort as she turned the deadbolt. The living room window was a gaping hole in the wall, along with a few other windows. The workers had put up some plastic sheeting over them, but the house wasn't exactly secure. Locking the door wasn't going to change anything.

With one last sad glance towards her broken security camera — she really should get on replacing that — she picked up Amaretto's carrier again and loaded the cat into the truck. Her house might not be secure, but at least she had everything important with her. She was glad Violet had offered up her couch for the night; she wouldn't have been comfortable sleeping here with the work on the windows only half-finished even if Amaretto escaping wasn't a concern.

She ran through her list of overnight items in her mind one last time to make sure she wasn't forgetting anything, then put her truck into reverse, only to slam her foot down on the brakes a second later when she spotted a person in her rearview mirror.

Undoing her seatbelt and putting the truck back into park in one motion, she opened the driver's door and got out.

"Jeeze, Beth. I almost ran you over. You just about gave me a heart attack."

The older woman looked chagrined. She let

Sammy, her Basset hound, tug forward on his leash to sniff at Flora's legs. She bent down to stroke his long, soft ears.

"Sorry about that. I thought you'd seen me waving," Beth said. "I was just on one of my regular walks when I saw you packing your things into your truck. Is everything all right?"

"Yeah, I'm just spending the night away from home because the work on the windows is taking longer than I expected. I'll be back tomorrow."

"Oh, good. I was a little worried when I saw you packing up out of the blue like that."

"Sorry to worry you, but thanks for coming to check up on me," Flora said. She meant it — slowly but surely, she was getting used to how involved Beth liked to be in her life. The older woman meant well, and she was genuinely kind in a way that most people weren't, even if she could be a little overbearing at times.

"Of course, dear. You have a nice night. I'd better head for home. I'm expecting another grocery delivery soon. It's so wonderful to be able to get fresh groceries whenever I need them."

Flora smiled as she got back into her truck, glad that Beth had discovered a service that gave her a little more freedom. It must have been hard for the older woman to be unable to drive in such a rural setting.

She waited until Beth and Sammy were safely out of the way before pulling out of the driveway and heading towards town. It would be nice to spend the evening with Violet, and tomorrow, the rest of the windows would be put in and if she was lucky, she might even finish painting her kitchen.

The storm might have brought more than its share of troubles, but things were looking up.

Flora woke the next morning to a familiar weight on her stomach, on an unfamiliar couch. It took her a moment to remember that she was at Violet's. She craned her neck down to see Amaretto curled up on top of her, snoozing away peacefully. The cat had settled in quickly; it probably helped that Amaretto knew and liked Violet, so all of the scents here were familiar and calming. They had spent a fun evening watching movies and eating takeout, with the cat joining them out of her hiding spot only halfway through.

When Violet's bedroom door opened, Flora realized her friend's alarm going off must have been what woke her up. She sat up on the couch, shifting the cat off of her, and opened her mouth to greet the other woman, only to have to cover an unexpected yawn instead.

Violet gave a drowsy chuckle. "Sorry if I woke you," she said quietly. "I love my job, but boy does it require early mornings."

"It's all right," Flora said. "I'm sure a lot of people are glad they can get their morning fix of caffeine bright and early. Though, I don't think any amount of coffee could make me want to get up at this hour every day."

Her friend snorted and stepped into the small kitchen to start her espresso machine. "Luckily, I am a natural morning person, but this schedule was hard even for me at first. You're welcome to go back to sleep once I leave, if you want. Just lock the door behind you when I go — I'll leave a spare key on the counter for you. Oh, and you're welcome to leave your cat here for the day, if you think she'd be less stressed here than she would be at your place with the workers. You can pick her up whenever they're done."

"Are you sure? I appreciate it. I'd have to lock her in my basement otherwise, and she's not a fan of that."

Despite how early it was, Flora found herself unable to doze off again after Violet left to open her coffee shop. She gave up around seven and packed her things back into her overnight bag, then fed Amaretto and made sure the cat had been using the litter box she had set up in the bathroom.

"You're going to stay here today, sweetie," she said. "I'll pick you up this evening once all of the work on the house is done."

While the cat was distracted with her breakfast, Flora grabbed the key off the counter in the kitchen and stepped out of the apartment, locking the door behind her. The people from the window company weren't supposed to arrive until between eight and nine, so she had about an hour to go home, shower, and make some breakfast before they arrived. She wasn't in a hurry, but she didn't have much time to waste either. Hopping into her truck, she started the engine and headed for home.

It was a little strange to be pulling up to her house so early in the morning. She didn't often get to see it in the early dawn light. Maybe it was just because it had sat empty all night, but she thought it looked oddly lonely like this, silhouetted against the dawn sky without any vehicles in the driveway or lights on.

She pulled up to her normal spot close to the house, sparing a thought of appreciation for the new gravel and the lack of potholes before she grabbed her purse and her overnight bag and got out of her vehicle.

The plastic covering over the living room window was flapping in the breeze as she walked up the porch steps. It must have come loose in the night. Thankfully, it hadn't rained, so at most a few bugs had gotten inside. Learning to live with creepy-crawlies constantly trying to invade her house was one of the more difficult aspects of adjusting to life in the country. Hopefully getting the windows replaced would help with that issue, as well as keeping the interior of the house better insulated.

She unlocked the door and pushed it open, only for it to bump up against something before it could open fully. Frowning, she pushed against it. Whatever had blocked the door shifted enough that she could slip in through the gap. She was trying to remember if the window repair team had left any rolls of plastic or other supplies in the front entrance way as she slipped through.

What she saw on the other side froze her in her tracks. The object that was blocking the door wasn't a roll of plastic or heavy bag of tools.

It was a body. A body she recognized. Tucker, one of the young men she had hired to pick up sticks in her yard, was lying dead in her foyer.

CHAPTER FIVE

Flora's scream caught in her throat. For a long moment, she felt completely frozen, unable to even breathe. A thud made her jump, and she realized it was just her purse falling to the floor — she had dropped it without realizing.

The sound seemed to snap her out of the shock that had frozen her. Carefully, she slipped the rest of the way inside and crouched next to the body. And there was no question it was a body — Tucker was long dead, his eyes open and blank, and dried blood crusted around a wound at the back of his head. Lying on the floor a few feet away, she saw the table lamp from the living room, the shade crumpled and the base of it bent.

She was no expert, but what had happened

seemed obvious. Someone had used her lamp to kill Tucker.

When she realized that crouching on the floor and staring at the scene wasn't going to achieve anything, she took her cell phone out of her jeans' back pocket and dialed 911.

When the police arrived, they came in through the back door so as not to disturb the scene by the front entrance. Flora had the inane urge to apologize for her half-painted kitchen, but bit her tongue and hung back until Officer Hendricks gestured for her to follow him outside. He looked grim. While he might joke and occasionally tease her about her penchant for stumbling across trouble, she knew this was serious, and they were both treating it as such.

"While my colleagues go over the scene, why don't you tell me what happened?" he asked once they were out of the way of the investigators who were going in and out through the mudroom entrance. He clicked a pen open and held it poised over a notepad.

"I... I have no idea," she said. She had to pause to clear her throat. None of this felt real, not yet, though she knew it would hit her soon. "I hired him to pick up sticks from the storm. I don't know why he was in my house. I wasn't even here!"

"Ms. Abner, please take a moment to breathe. I'm aware that this is hard for you. There's no rush. Why don't you start with how you knew Tucker Franks?"

Flora took several deep, slow breaths, then started to explain how Tucker and Duncan worked for her neighbor, and how she had come to decide to hire them after the storm. That led to her telling Officer Hendricks about the broken window and spending the night at Violet's rather than in the house when the window company was only half-done installing the new windows.

By the time she reached the part of her story where she discovered the body, she was feeling a little better, or at least less like she was drowning in the horror of it all.

"He should have been long gone," she finished. "He and Duncan only had an hour's worth of work left to do when I left last night."

"Were they aware that you were going to be gone all night?" he asked.

"Yeah. I told them I'd rather pay them then even though they hadn't quite finished yet, since I wouldn't be back until mid-morning." She paused. "Wait, do you think they took the opportunity to break in, since they knew I'd be gone all night?"

"It's too early to be certain of anything. I'm just

trying to learn what information the involved parties had. Who else knew you would be gone overnight?"

"My neighbor, Beth, and the friend I stayed with, of course." She frowned, wracking her mind. "Um, I texted another friend, Linus Kade, to let him know I might not be able to make our lunch date today since I would have the window people here again and would be spending the night at Violet's and probably getting a slow start. I think that's it."

She hadn't told Grady simply because it was so much easier to text someone quickly than it was to call them, and the man *still* didn't have a cell phone.

She watched as Officer Hendricks made notes. After a moment, she took a breath. "What happens now?"

"Well, I'm going to make some calls and confirm your alibi with your friend." He must have seen the look on her face because his grim expression turned a little kinder. "I don't believe you were involved in this, Ms. Abner, but I wouldn't be much of an investigator if I didn't follow protocol just because I've gotten to know you decently well over the past few months."

"Thanks," she said. "I understand."

"I'll also be requesting the footage from your security cameras. With a little luck and some good video footage, this should be an open and shut case."

She grimaced. "About that… the front camera was fried when the power went out during the storm, and I haven't gotten around to replacing it yet. The back one still works, though, and you're welcome to that footage."

He sighed. "That's a shame, but it can't be helped. I'll have another officer escort you into the house so you can pack. If I'm remembering correctly, you have a cat. Will you need help catching her?"

"I do have a cat, but she's already at Violet's. I figured it would be less stressful for her if I left her there for the day, rather than bringing her back here with all of the noise and chaos that will come when the window installation resumes." Her eyes widened. "Shoot. I've got to call them and tell them they're going to need to come back later. Hold on, why would I have to pack?"

"Your home is a crime scene, Ms. Abner," Officer Hendricks said gently. "You'll need to vacate the premises for a few days while the forensics team goes over everything. Do you have somewhere to stay?"

Flora sighed. "I'll figure it out. I'd better call the window company now; they're supposed to be here soon."

"Pack first," he said, waving a younger officer over. "We'll handle it if they show up in the meantime. While you're gathering your things, take a look through the rest of the house as well, and note down anything that seems to be missing. This isn't just a homicide; the victim and killer were both breaking and entering, and it's possible the killer took something with them when they left."

With that thought in her head, she allowed the younger officer to lead her away. Her first stop was in the kitchen, to stock up on Amaretto's cans of fancy cat food, then to her bedroom to get some more clothes. Nothing seemed to be disturbed, but then, she didn't keep many valuables in the house.

Tucker and his killer must have been disappointed when they broke in and found that there was nothing to steal but some clothing and dishes and self-assembled furniture.

Loaded down with bags, she left through the back door, pausing only to give Officer Hendricks the login information for her security camera. It felt odd and a little unpleasant to be kicked out of her own house, but she didn't exactly want to hang around with a dead body there anyway, so she loaded her things into her truck without comment.

She probably shouldn't have been surprised when

she heard Beth's familiar, "Yoo-hoo!" from down the road. Of course the older woman would have walked over to see what all of the commotion was about.

Slamming the truck's door shut, she walked out onto the dirt road to meet her neighbor. Beth looked her up and down before making an exaggerated noise of relief.

"Thank goodness you're all right, dear. When I saw the police cars, I was so worried. Whatever happened?"

"Someone broke into my house while I was gone last night," Flora said. "Then something else must have happened, because I found their body inside."

She kept it vague on purpose; she didn't want word about Tucker getting out before the police had time to notify his family.

"Oh, my. How horrible." The older woman shuddered. "Thank goodness you were gone."

Flora wondered if the break-in would still have happened if she was there. Maybe she *was* lucky not to be there. The thought made her shiver.

"I'll stop in to chat with you in a day or two. Right now, I kind of want to get going. Maybe you could go chat with the police? If you saw or heard anything last night, it might help them."

"Of course." Beth gave a firm nod, her eyes glinting. The older woman would never admit it, but this sort of thing was right up her alley. She loved a good chance to gossip, even if the people she was talking to were in uniform. "But why are you leaving, dear? Where are you going?"

"They need me to be off the property while they look for evidence," she said. "I'm not sure yet where I'll go; maybe to Violet's, or maybe to the motel."

"If you want to come stay with me, you're welcome," Beth said. "And your cat, too. We have a lovely guest room you could stay in."

Flora considered the offer for a moment, but then shook her head. "Thank you, Beth. I really appreciate it, but I don't think Amaretto would appreciate being around Sammy. She's never lived with a dog before, and I'm worried she would be terrified. She might even be scared enough to find a way outside, and I'm not sure what would happen to her then."

"I understand. If you change your mind, just let me know."

Flora promised she would, and watched as Beth approached one of the officers to ask if she could be of help, then she got into her truck. She would have to talk to Violet about staying at her place for another night or two, but that wasn't her biggest concern right now.

She couldn't stop wondering how things had gone so wrong for poor Tucker. It was hard to hate him for breaking into her house while she was gone when he had faced the ultimate consequence for his actions. Someone had killed him, and the questions of *who* and *why* were going to drive her crazy.

CHAPTER SIX

When Flora swung by the coffee shop to tell Violet about the horrible surprise that had been waiting for her at home, her friend was flabbergasted by the news.

"Flora, I swear you have the worst luck of anyone I've ever met. Of course you can keep staying with me. You still have the key, right? Feel free to let yourself back in and make yourself at home. I'll come home right after I'm done here and we can talk more."

"Thanks, Violet. I owe you for this."

"Don't be silly. You'd do the same for me." Her friend paused to run the coffee grinder behind the counter and wrinkled her nose when she looked back up. "Not that I'd need it... seriously, stop finding bodies, okay? It can't be good for your health."

"It's not like I do it on purpose," Flora grumbled. "I feel so horrible. I know Tucker wasn't supposed to be in my house and whatever reason he had for being there probably wasn't great, but he didn't deserve to *die*. I'd rather he had managed to successfully rob me blind, instead of what happened. I can replace *things*. He had a whole life ahead of him, and now all of that is just... gone."

"I know." Violet sighed, then turned to glance at the door as someone came in. "Look, I want to talk about this more, I really do, but I'm the only one working this morning and it's been busy. We'll talk this evening, okay? I promise."

"All right. I'll go mope around at your apart-ment." Flora straightened up from where she had been leaning on the counter, then paused. "Actually, could you get me my regular order, and something for Grady too? I need to tell him what happened, and I don't really want to be alone right now, so I think I'm going to go hang around the hardware store for a while."

"Sure thing," Violet said, reaching for a cup to start on Flora's usual white chocolate caramel latte.

"It'll even be on the house today. Consider it the trauma discount."

Flora snorted despite herself and gratefully accepted the drinks from her friend a couple of minutes later. She made the short drive to the hardware store and carried the two cups inside, pausing to shout a greeting to old Mr. Brant, the hard of hearing proprietor of the store.

Grady walked past her carrying heavy bags of sand for an older woman who was chattering at him a mile a minute. He gave Flora a smile in greeting, and she leaned against the wall to wait for him to be done helping the customer. His boss didn't mind her spending time at the hardware store as long as they weren't too busy and she didn't get in the way.

After the woman paid for the bags of sand, he carried them outside and then re-entered the store, taking his cup of coffee from her gratefully.

"This is a nice surprise," he said. "Do you need to buy something, or are you just stopping by?"

"The latter," she said. "It's not just a social visit, though. A lot has happened since the last time we talked."

They made their way out to the hardware shop's small garden center and sat at one of the wicker display tables with their coffee, and Flora told him everything that had happened the day before and that morning, from the decision to spend the night at Violet's, to leaving while Tucker and Duncan were still at her house, to finding Tucker's body and calling the police earlier that morning.

His sharp look of concern was unsurprising. Talking to him made it feel more real, and by the time her story ended, she was slumped in her seat.

"I feel so guilty, like maybe he would still be alive if I hadn't decided to go to Violet's last night, or if I hadn't told them I would be gone until morning."

"It's not your fault," he told her. "He chose to break into your house. It was his own decision that led to what happened, not yours."

"Yeah, but he didn't deserve to *die* for it," she said. "He was so young, Grady. Like, college age, or maybe just out of high school. Heck, for all I know, he wasn't even breaking in to steal something, he just wanted to poke around an old, empty house at night."

"I feel bad for the kid," Grady said after a moment. "But I'm more worried that whoever killed him is still out there and got a chance to learn the layout of your house. Whoever it is probably knows you live alone. They know where everything that can be used as a weapon is in your house. They know what room you sleep in. You don't know what they want. It isn't safe."

Flora shuddered. "You're acting like this was someone who targeted me on purpose," she said. "It was probably just a random break-in. Tucker and Duncan knew I was going to be gone all night and they knew my house was easy to get into. Something just… went wrong between them. Who knows, maybe they were going to steal the table lamp and Duncan tripped and hit Tucker with it accidentally."

Grady raised an eyebrow, looking unimpressed. "You know that sounds ridiculous, don't you?"

Flora sighed. "All right, sure. It is ridiculous. But it doesn't change the fact that Duncan is probably the one who killed Tucker, and they were probably just there because the house was convenient. It doesn't have anything to do with me, personally."

"That might be true," he relented. "But it's a lot of 'probablys.' What if you're wrong? I hate the thought of you being there alone after this."

"Well, it's going to be a few days, at the very least, before I can go back," she said with a sigh. "By the time I return, I'm pretty sure the police will have arrested Duncan and it won't be a concern anymore.

What I *will* do is buy a new security camera while I'm here. That way, if something goes wrong in the investigation or the police think Duncan wasn't involved, I'll have advance notice if the killer comes back."

After they finished their coffee and their discussion, Flora picked out a new security camera and Grady walked with her to the check out. She felt a little bad that he was so worried, but the case seemed clear cut to her. What happened to Tucker was horrible, but even though it had happened at her house, it wasn't *about* her.

She wouldn't feel completely safe in her house for a while, but that was just because she was shaken by the experience. She didn't think she was in any danger. She knew Grady meant well, but sometimes he worried too much.

He walked her out to her truck after she paid, and she gave him a brief hug goodbye. "We still have to plan out our next date," she said. "Maybe the day after tomorrow? We could get dinner when you're done working."

"There's no rush," he assured her. "But that works for me. Just… be careful in the meantime, okay? I know you don't think there's anything to worry about, but humor me."

"I will," she assured him. She left him with a

quick peck on his cheek, and got into her truck, almost heading towards home automatically before remembering that she was currently staying with Violet. She drove towards her friend's apartment instead, trying to put the unsettling conversation with Grady out of her mind.

CHAPTER SEVEN

Flora woke bright and early once again the next morning, a consequence of the early hours Violet kept. She waved off her friend's apologies when Violet came into the living room to find she had woken Flora once again.

"I don't mind," she promised. "Besides, I don't have anything else to do today. I can't go home yet, and it's not like I can work remotely."

"You know, I never thought I'd know someone who was as eager to get back to their job as you are," her friend said, sounding amused. "What are you going to do to entertain yourself all day?"

"Well, I'm going to call Officer Hendricks and see if he has any updates. Maybe I'll get lucky and they will have finished at my house early. After that..."

She trailed off and shrugged. "I couldn't say. Maybe I'll go to the library and find some books to read. Or if you wanted, I could come help out at the coffee shop. I worked as a barista for a semester in college, I could probably manage to be at least a little useful."

Her friend laughed. "Well, if you want to come in and help, I won't stop you. Don't feel like you have to, though."

"I want to," Flora said firmly. "You're letting Amaretto and me stay here even though, according to Grady, there could be a crazed killer after me. It's the least I can do."

"Grady only worries so much because he cares," Violet said. She tugged her boots on, bending over to lace them. "I'd better get going. Swing by whenever you want, and I'll find something for you to do. Have a good day until then."

"You too," Flora said. "I'll see you later."

She knew she shouldn't call Officer Hendricks until eight-thirty or nine at the earliest, so she spent some time on her normal morning routine, and then worked on training her cat. She hadn't thought to bring Amaretto's harness from her house, but she *had* brought the cat treats, so she spent some time getting the cat to jump between two of the tall kitchen barstools Violet owned, gradually increasing the distance between them as the cat got more confident.

Finally, she deemed it late enough to bother Officer Hendricks, and sat down on the couch with her cell phone in her hand. She had his number saved, and only had to tap on the screen twice to send the call through. He answered after just a couple of rings.

"Good morning, Ms. Abner. I'm hoping this is you calling for an update rather than to report yet another issue."

"It's your lucky day," she said. "Have you made any progress? Can I go home yet? Did you arrest Duncan?"

"It's an ongoing case," he said, sounding tired. "No arrests have been made yet, but I've got to tell you, I don't think Duncan Fowler is our guy. He has an alibi that seems pretty solid. I need to send some men to comb through your house again today. I can't be certain when you'll be able to return, but I promise you, I don't want to keep you from your home any more than you want to be kept from it."

"I know," she said with a sigh. "Thanks for the update, at least. You're sure it isn't Duncan?"

"You know I can't go into detail," he said. "But if you can think of anyone else who knew your house would be empty that night, I would appreciate their names."

"I'll have to think about it," she said. "Beth and Violet are the only two that come to mind, and I already told you about them. And I think we both know Beth didn't have anything to do with it, and Violet was at work all day."

"You mentioned someone else as well." She heard the sound of him shuffling through papers. "A Linus Kade?"

"Well, sure, I told Linus too, but he's a friend of mine. I don't think he had anything to do with it either."

"I see," Officer Hendricks said. "Well, I'd best get back to work. Thank you for calling, Flora. I'll update you if we have anything new to report."

They said their goodbyes and he ended the call. Flora put her phone down slowly, feeling both frustrated and a little worried. If they weren't arresting Duncan, and he had a solid alibi, then who had been in the house with Tucker? She'd been so certain it was Duncan, but now it seemed that Grady had been right after all.

If the killer *wasn't* Duncan but had known she would be gone that night, it narrowed down the list of people who might be involved considerably, but it raised some other questions. Why would someone want to break into her house? She could accept that Tucker, or Tucker and Duncan, had done it just for the kicks, because they were young and knew she would be gone and wanted to poke through the house. She didn't like that Tucker had broken in, but his death was a lot more important to her than whatever items he might have been there to steal.

But if there *was* another person involved, someone who wasn't Duncan, who wasn't Tucker's friend, what was *their* reason for breaking in? Were they looking to steal her belongings… or were they looking for *her*?

Try as she might, she couldn't think of anyone who was out for her blood, so she decided to focus on the former option first, which meant figuring out who, exactly, had known she was going to be gone. She decided to start with Linus, since she was in town already and they already had loose plans to meet for lunch. She didn't think he had been involved on purpose, but it was possible he had mentioned her issues with the house's windows to another friend.

She checked her messages from him. She didn't have any new texts besides the one he had sent her the day before in acknowledgment of her canceling their get-together. She sent off a quick text saying, *Are we still on for lunch today?*

She decided to call Beth while she waited for a reply. The older woman sounded surprised to hear from her when she answered.

"Flora? Is everything all right, dear?"

"Everything is fine, Beth," she said. "I just had a few questions for you. Do you have a minute to talk?"

"Of course. What do you need?"

"Two days ago, when I told you I was going to be spending the night away from home, did you happen to tell anyone else about that? Any of your friends, or other neighbors?"

"I'm hurt that you think I spend all of my time gossiping," Beth said. "Really, Flora. I'm not *that* chatty."

"Can you just answer the question, Beth?" she asked. "It's important."

The older woman was silent for a moment. "Well, no, I don't think I mentioned it to anyone. I suppose I might have said something to Natalie when she came over later that evening to return my vase, but that was only because she asked me how the work on your windows was going. I think she's considering hiring the same company to work on some of her windows."

"Just her? No one else?" Flora asked.

"I don't think so. It's not as if I update every one of my friends every time you leave the house, dear."

Flora sighed, not sure if she should be relieved or disappointed. As much as Natalie didn't like her, she didn't think the other woman had been involved in Tucker's death. Natalie resented her for Flora's part in her brother's arrest, but that didn't mean she wanted to see Flora dead, right? And she didn't have a reason to murder one of the people who she had hired, either.

"Oh, hold on," Beth said. "When Nolan came over with the groceries, I thanked him for being such a dear, and I told him how much the grocery service meant to me, and how vulnerable I often feel all alone out here with Tim as he is, and especially when you're not home. You might not realize this, but I rely on you and value your friendship, Flora. It comforts me to know you're always just a minute away if I need something."

So Beth *had* told someone else, but not anyone who would have a reason to want to hurt her. She could give Officer Hendricks Nolan's name, but unless he had a criminal history, she didn't think it would do much good.

"I'm glad you feel safer with me nearby, and you know I'm always happy to help you and Tim with anything you need," she said. "Thanks for answering my questions, Beth. I'll let you go now."

Her phone buzzed with an incoming text message while Beth was still saying goodbye. Flora patiently waited until they ended the call, then checked her messages to see a new text from Linus.

Sure. Sandwich shop at noon?

She replied with a, *Sounds good!* then looked down at Amaretto, who had settled herself on Flora's lap.

"I'm going to head to the coffee shop," she told the cat as she ran her fingers through Amaretto's soft fur. I'll see you later. You be good here, okay?"

The cat purred in response. Flora left a couple of extra treats in the cat bowl before gathering her things and heading out the door.

CHAPTER EIGHT

She spent a couple of hours before noon helping Violet out around the coffee shop. She was relegated to getting people drip coffee, refilling the napkin dispensers, and washing dirty dishes, but she didn't mind. She enjoyed helping her friend out, and it was easy work.

She left shortly before noon to meet Linus, with a promise to bring Violet a sandwich back for lunch. The sandwich shop was only a short drive away, and she was looking forward to the meal even if she wasn't looking forward to telling Linus about what had happened. Unlike the rest of her friend group, she didn't know him particularly well yet. He had moved to town only a couple of months ago, and had given her his number back when he was looking for a job and was hoping she could be of help. Both of them had been busy, and they had only managed to get together one other time since then. He seemed like a nice guy, she just wasn't thrilled about having to share the horrifying experience of finding Tucker's body with someone who was more of a friendly acquaintance than a true friend. But she needed answers. She needed to get Officer Hendricks a list of the names of everyone who had known she was going to be gone that night. Only then would she let herself look into the more frightening possibility; that whoever had killed Tucker wasn't at her house to burglarize it, but instead was there to kill her.

Linus was waiting in the parking lot for her. He got out of his car when he saw her park her truck, and she greeted him with a wave, hoping the stress of the last couple of days didn't show on her face.

"Hey," he said. "Everything going all right with the windows?"

"It's complicated," she told him, wrinkling her nose. "Let's go in and order, and I'll tell you all about it."

They went inside and ordered their sandwiches, Flora ordering one to go for Violet as well. They found a table to sit at while they waited for the sandwiches to be made, and Flora got down to business.

"So, that night I was gone, someone broke into my house," she said.

"No kidding," he said, his eyes wide. "That's terrible. They didn't take anything important, did they?

"No, or at least not that I've noticed," she said. "But that's not the worst part. One of the burglars was killed, and I found his body the next morning."

He sat back in his chair, blinking.

"That's horrible, Flora," he breathed. I'm so sorry you had to go through that. Have you been staying somewhere else? Do they know who killed him?"

"I've been staying with –" She was about to say with Violet, but cut herself off at the last minute. She didn't think Linus had anything to do with this, but being cautious wouldn't hurt. "I've been staying with a friend," she said instead. He didn't know her well enough to immediately guess who that was, though Grady or Sydney would have known she meant Violet in a heartbeat. "I'm safe, but no, they don't know who did it. The only suspect they had has an alibi, apparently. I'm trying to get a list of the people who knew I would be gone to give to one of the investigators in the case. Did you happen to tell anyone that I was going to be spending the night away from home that evening?"

"Who would I tell?" he asked, sounding confused. "I barely know anyone in town other than you. And speaking of, I hope we can have another lunch date soon. Or maybe we could get dinner? It's nice to have someone to talk to, and I'd love to be a friendly ear while you're going through all of this. It can't be easy."

"Yeah," she said with a sigh. "Thanks, Linus. You're absolutely sure you didn't mention it to anyone, though?"

He shook his head and mimed zipping his lips shut. "I didn't tell a soul."

She was in a somber mood when she took Violet her sandwich. Neither of her conversations had been enlightening, and she had a bad feeling that she had done as much as she could to help with this case. It was time for her to sit back and wait for the police to do their jobs. Which, no offense to Officer Hendricks and his coworkers, was something she absolutely hated doing. She trusted that they would get the killer eventually, but she liked being proactive. It didn't sit right with her to do nothing but wait.

After handing the sandwich off to Violet, she promised her friend she would come back out front to help again soon, then stepped into the small kitchen to call Officer Hendricks. She told him what Beth had told her about mentioning her absence to both Natalie and Nolan, and then how Linus had promised he hadn't said word to anyone. Officer Hendricks thanked her and told her he was noting the names down, but didn't offer her any more news on the progress of the case.

After she ended the call, she returned to the main part of the coffee shop. It was just after lunchtime and the middle of a lull in business, so she took the opportunity to chat with Violet while her friend ate. She told the other woman how her day had gone, and about her lunch meeting with Linus.

"I bet Grady won't be happy to hear about that," her friend said with a chuckle.

"What do you mean?" Flora asked.

"Well, I know you're not, like, dating Linus, but that's probably how it seems to an outside observer."

Flora leaned back against the counter, rolling her eyes. "This is the second time I've gotten together with him. I'm just spending time with him because we're both newcomers here. Not that there's anything wrong with hanging out with you, Sydney, and Grady, but Linus understands how hard it can be to move to a small town like this."

"Does Linus know that?" Violet asked. "Because

when a pretty girl accepts his invitation out to a meal…"

"I'm starting to think you don't believe men and women can just be friends."

"I think *you're* a little too focused on your house to notice certain obvious things," Violet said.

Flora sighed decided to change the subject. "Speaking of guys, how are things with Sydney going?"

"Good," Violet said. "We're casually seeing each other, I'm not sure –"

She broke off when the coffee shop door opened. Flora looked up too, ready to get back to work if she was needed.

The man who came in had a baseball cap pulled low over his head and walked with his face tucked down, so she didn't recognize him until he reached the counter and looked up at the menu. When she did, her fingers tightened on the edge of the counter, and she took in a deep breath.

Duncan. Tucker's business partner, and the man she still thought was the most obvious suspect in his murder. If the way he was trying to hide his appearance was any hint, she wasn't the only one who thought that. In a town this small, a lot of people must know about his friendship with Tucker. She wondered what his friends and family thought, if they believed he was innocent.

She also wondered what his alibi was. Had he gotten someone to lie for him? She was sure the police would have thought of that, of course, but he seemed like *such* an obvious suspect. She wished the case was as cut and dry as it had seemed at the beginning.

"Welcome to Violet Delights," Violet said. "What can I get you today?"

"I'll have a medium…" His eyes flicked to Flora and he trailed off. She gulped, realizing he had recognized her. His face paled.

"Never mind, I don't think I'll get anything after all."

With that, he turned and hurried away from the counter, pushing through the door and vanishing down the sidewalk. Flora and Violet both stared after him, until Flora turned to face her friend.

"I'd apologize for driving your customers away, but I'm still eighty percent sure he murdered his friend, so…"

Violet shook her head slowly. "Only you, Flora. When I tell you your life is interesting, I don't mean it as a compliment."

CHAPTER NINE

Officer Hendricks had promised to call her when he had an update as to when she could go back to her house, so she refrained from calling him the next morning. Lacking anything better to do, she went into work with Violet and helped her open the coffee shop. While she wouldn't want to wake up this early every day, it was fun to spend the morning with her friend – and the free latte Violet offered her didn't hurt either. She loved working on her house, but there was something to be said for the cozy, welcoming atmosphere Violet's coffee shop boasted. She knew many of her customers quite well, and the morning was filled with pleasant chit-chat. Flora heard a few people ask if Violet had heard about the recent murder, but thankfully, no one seemed to recognize her or connect her to the case.

After helping Violet close the coffee shop that afternoon, they returned to her apartment. Amaretto had made herself at home there over the past couple of days, and greeted Flora and Violet at the door confidently, twining her tail around their ankles as she rubbed against their shins.

Flora spent a few minutes chatting to her cat and stroking her fluffy fur while Violet made some relaxing tea to share. Her friend's apartment wasn't anywhere near as large as Flora's apartment back in Chicago had been, but it was cozy and comfortable. She enjoyed being there, and was glad Violet had been so kind in letting her and her cat stay there. While she was eager to get back to her own house, she would be a lot more desperate if she was staying at the local motel instead of here.

"What time are you meeting Grady?" Violet asked as they settled onto the couch.

"Well, he gets out of work at seven. He's going to call me after he gets home and changes, but I'll probably meet him around eight."

"This is, what, your second date?"

"Yeah, though we've gone out to eat together plenty in the past," she said.

"True, but it's different when both parties *realize* it's a date."

"I just hope things get back to normal between us soon. It's been a little awkward ever since we first went out."

"They will," Violet assured her. "You're just figuring out how your new relationship is going to work. So, what are you going to wear?"

Flora opened her mouth, then closed it again with a click of her teeth. "Shoot. I left all of my good clothes at home. Maybe I should call Officer Hendricks after all, and ask if I can stop by to get some clothing.

"Don't bother doing that, just borrow something of mine."

"Are you sure?"

"Of course," Violet said, getting up. "Come on, let's look through my closet and see what you like."

Flora ended up borrowing a pair of leggings and a comfortable, extra-long shirt to go over them. They fit her well enough and they were a lot nicer than any of the clothes she had brought with her in her hurried packing when she left her house.

She liked a lot of things about Warbler, but it was lacking any really nice restaurants. For their first date, they had gone to one of the local restaurants, but this time around they were going to a steakhouse a little ways outside of town. Grady offered to pick her up when he called to let her know he was done with work, and she got into his old pickup truck while Violet waved from the apartment window above them.

"Have the two of you been having a good time together?" he asked as he drove out of town.

"We are," she said. "Don't get me wrong, I miss my home, but it's been nice staying with her and I'm glad she offered."

"Do you know yet when you'll be able to go home?"

She sighed. "Not yet. Officer Hendricks said he would call me when he knows something. I haven't spoken to him since yesterday, though. I might have to give in and call him tomorrow."

"The company hasn't been able to finish installing the windows either?"

She wrinkled her nose. "Unfortunately, no. I'm just hoping the police presence will keep anyone else from breaking in – and that they would let me know if I had an invasion of raccoons or stray cats or something making themselves at home."

"I'm sure you'll be able to return soon," he said as he put a blinker on to make a turn. "They can't keep you away forever." In the rearview mirror, Flora saw the car behind them make the same turn. She didn't think anything of it, not until the vehicle followed them for the next two turns in a row. When she noticed that, she touched Grady's arm.

"Does it seem weird to you that the car that's behind us has been following us since we left town?"

She saw him glance in the mirror. He shrugged.

"There aren't that many roads out of town. They're probably heading to the next town over, just like we are."

She glanced at the car in the mirror again and told herself she was just being paranoid. Tucker's death had made her hyper aware of her surroundings, that was all.

But the vehicle kept following them, all the way to the restaurant. It turned into the parking lot right after they did, and Flora couldn't take her eyes off it in the rearview mirror.

"Okay, they are definitely following us."

Grady was frowning too. He parked towards the back of the lot, and Flora was mildly relieved when the other vehicle took a spot closer to the restaurant's entrance instead.

"We'll be careful," he said. "Let's head inside for now."

Flora picked up her purse and got out of his truck. He paused to lock the doors – not something he normally bothered doing in Warbler – and then stayed close to her as they headed up towards the entrance. Whoever had been following them must have already gone inside, because no one was waiting for them at the entrance. They went in and spoke to the hostess, who was able to seat them immediately. As they walked to their table, Flora looked around, but didn't see anyone who looked familiar. At least, not until the last person she had expected to see there called out her name.

"Flora! What a surprise."

Surprise was definitely the word for it. She shared a puzzled look with Grady as Linus waved at them from a two-person table in the far corner, then got up to greet them. The hostess seated them and left while Linus was still standing by their table.

"It's good to see you too, Linus," Flora said once she had gotten past the worst of her surprise. "What are you doing here?

"Oh, I have a date," he said. "I think she's running late, though. Are you here on a date as well?" He glanced at Grady. "I didn't know you were seeing someone."

"Yeah, I've known Grady for a while," she said.

74

"Were you the one who was behind us all the way from town?"

"If you were the ones in the pickup truck, then yep, that was me," he said, chuckling. "Small world, isn't it?"

"Definitely," she said.

She picked up her menu, hoping he would get the message that she was ready to focus on her meal with Grady, but he kept talking.

"You've got to tell me how you make friends so quickly," he said. "It seems like everyone around town knows you."

She looked up at that. "What do you mean?"

"Well, when I was at work earlier today, Sydney came in to pick up some groceries," he said. He had attended one of Flora's bonfires a few weeks ago, and had met her friends, though they hadn't had the chance to all get together again. "He asked how I was doing, then asked if I'd heard what happened to you. One of my coworkers overheard him and asked if we knew you. I assumed he was a friend of yours, since he knew what happened to that poor young man at your house."

"What was his name?" she asked sharply.

He frowned. "A newer guy named Nolan. He just started recently, and does the new grocery deliveries."

"I've met him, but I don't *know* him. What all did he say?"

"He wanted to know how the police investigation was going. I told him you were hopeful you'd be able to move back in soon, but didn't know much other than that. Did I do something wrong?"

"No," she said slowly. "I'm just a little confused as to why he was asking about that. Anyway, I hope your date goes well."

"Thanks," he said. "I'll let you to get back to yours. It was nice seeing you, Flora."

He walked away at last, returning to his empty table. Flora gazed after him for a moment, considering what he had said. What was Nolan's interest in her? She had only met him once, in passing... though, knowing Beth, the older woman has probably told him all about her without thinking twice about it.

"You okay?" Grady asked. "You seem lost in thought."

"I'm not sure," she said. "You don't happen to know this Nolan guy at all, do you?"

Grady shook his head. "I don't have a clue who he is. Are you still trying to figure out who broke in?"

She nodded. "Yeah. If the police are right and Duncan is innocent, then narrowing down the list of people who knew I was going to be gone might help.

Of course, that's assuming the killer was another burglar. If they were there looking for *me,* then I don't even know where to start."

"Maybe it's a good thing you haven't been able to return home yet," he said. "At least if someone's after you, they don't know where to find you."

She supposed that was a silver lining, but it didn't change the fact that she missed her house, and she felt the time until Thanksgiving slipping away faster than ever. She wanted to impress her aunt, the woman who had made it possible for her to chase her dreams. If she couldn't even set foot inside her house, how in the world was she supposed to work on it?

CHAPTER TEN

It wasn't until after she and Grady were done splitting a slice of pecan pie that she realized Linus had left, and his date had never come.

Though she'd had a nice time on her date with Grady, she was mostly silent as they drove home, lost in thought once again. She had no reason to suspect Linus. He had never been anything but friendly to her, and he didn't have any motive to break into her house.

But... he had followed her and Grady to the restaurant. Sure, he had given them a reason, but had he been lying? Had his date stood him up, or had she not even existed in the first place? She hated that she even had to wonder about that. Why couldn't things be more simple?

"Sorry my life is so complicated," she told Grady as they approached Violet's apartment. "I had a really nice time tonight, though."

"I did too," he told her. After parking in front of the building, he got out of his truck and walked her to the door, where they paused for a moment and held each other's gazes uncertainly. Finally, he touched her cheek and gently kissed her on the lips. When she walked into Violet's apartment a minute later, she felt a little dazed, but happy. Linus' strange behavior aside, it had been a wonderful night.

She went to the coffee shop with Violet again the next morning, but kept her phone on her and waited impatiently for a call from Officer Hendricks. She was ready to get back to her life.

When lunchtime rolled around and he still hadn't called, she stepped into the kitchen and dialed his number. She couldn't stand not knowing what was going on.

He seemed distracted when he answered, but when she asked if she could return home yet, he said, "You should be good to go back tomorrow. I'll have an officer posted there today, so if you need to pick up some more things, feel free to swing by. I don't have any other updates to give you. We're working on a couple of angles, but we aren't going to have a resolution any time soon unless we get lucky and the perp confesses."

"Thanks," she said with a sigh. "At least I'll get to go home soon."

After work, she drove over to her house. It felt good to return after being gone for the past few days. The house looked the same as it had when she left it a few days ago, other than the police cruiser in her driveway. It was sitting empty, so she walked up the steps to the front porch and raised her knuckles to the door. It felt odd to knock on her own door, but she pushed the feeling aside as a familiar looking young policewoman opened it. Flora recognized her as the same woman who had driven her home when her purse was stolen not long ago.

She took Flora's name and looked at her driver's license, then told Flora she could gather whatever she needed.

"We're just doing one last sweep of the property today," she explained. "We should be out of here by tomorrow morning. I hope you're going to invest in some better security. You're pretty isolated out here."

"I already got a new camera to replace the broken one at the front door," Flora said. "Actually, I think it's still in the truck. Do you mind if I set it up today?"

"Feel free," the officer said. "I'm leaving in about forty minutes, so you have until then."

"Thanks," Flora said.

She grabbed the clothing she wanted, then took the new security camera out of her truck. It was the same model as the other one, so she already knew how to set it up. She had to remove the old one and secure the new one to the siding, then connect it to her Wi-Fi once it turned on. After that, she had to wait around for the software to update. The process took longer than she would have liked, but it was simple enough to do. She made sure she was getting the video feed on her phone, then breathed a quiet sigh of relief. At least she would have eyes on the front of her house again.

"I'm heading out," she said, sticking her head through the doorway to say goodbye to the police-woman. "Thanks for letting me set that camera up."

"No problem at all," she said. "Have a nice evening."

Flora shut the door behind her and went over to her truck, double checking that she had everything she needed. Finally, she got behind the wheel and put the vehicle into reverse, only to step on the brake when she spotted a van coming down the road.

It was Nolan's grocery delivery van. It drove

slowly past her house, and continued on past Beth's. She wondered if Natalie was getting groceries delivered now. It wouldn't surprise her; Natalie and Beth were getting closer, and Beth loved to recommend the things she enjoyed to her friends.

With the road behind her clear, she backed out of her driveway. When she got back to Violet's, she would call the window company and tell them they could resume service. With any luck, her life would start getting back to normal tomorrow.

CHAPTER ELEVEN

She was pleasantly surprised when the window company told her they would be at her house bright and early the next morning, and she and Violet ran out to the grocery store to pick up some wine and brownies for an impromptu celebration of her getting her life back in order.

She deliberated long and hard on the matter, but decided to help Violet at the coffee shop one last time instead of going straight home. Nothing against the window installation people, but she would rather be out of their hair while they worked, and she felt like she owed Violet.

To speed matters up a little, she woke earlier than usual the next morning to pack everything of hers from around Violet's apartment. She set Amaretto's cat carrier by the door, leaving the front open and tossing a few treats inside for the cat to find during the day. Amaretto wasn't a fan of the carrier, so hopefully she would build some good associations with it before it was time for Flora to put her in it.

"We're going home soon, sweetie," she said. "I hope you're as excited as I am."

She said goodbye to the cat and headed to the coffee shop, only a few minutes behind Violet. It was an overcast, windy morning, and walking into the rich scents and warm air inside Violet Delights felt like walking into a hug. Her good mood persisted as she helped Violet open and serve their first customers of the day.

A little after eight, her phone chimed with a notification from the video camera she had set up the day before. The words *Person detected at front door* nearly gave her a heart attack until she remembered the window installation people were coming. She checked the footage to make sure it was them and relaxed when she saw the familiar logos on their outfits. She was glad they had come so early; with a little luck, they would be all done with the windows by the time Flora left the coffee shop.

The notifications kept going off, and eventually

she muted her phone so she could concentrate on helping Violet with the coffee.

She stayed all the way until three, which was later than she had been planning on staying, but every time she glanced at her phone screen, she saw another notification of movement detected at the front door. That was enough to tell her that the workers were still there.

After they wiped down the counters and locked the doors, she took her phone off mute and checked her messages. Sydney had texted the group chat, asking if they wanted to have a bonfire this weekend, and she had a missed call from a local number. She listened to the voicemail and felt a rush of excitement at the news it contained.

"Hi, this is Bob Davis from Green Hills Glass. I'm calling to let you know we've finished the work on your house. I hope you enjoy your new windows."

As she pulled her phone away from her ear, she happened to glance at the screen and saw that the message had been left just after one. She had gotten a new notification from the front door camera just ten minutes ago, so who had set it off?

"Everything all right?" Violet asked.

"I think so," Flora said as she navigated to the

security cameras' app. "Sounds like the window people are done at my house."

"That's good," Violet said. "You must be happy."

"I am," she murmured, frowning as she waited for the footage to load. Finally, the video started playing. She saw her front porch, familiar and welcoming in the early fall sunlight. Someone climbed the steps, a bouquet of flowers in one hand.

It wasn't one of the employees from the window company. It was Linus. She watched as he knocked on the door, and then the video clip ended.

"Flora? Is something wrong?"

"Linus was at my house ten minutes ago," she said. "With… flowers."

"He saw you on a date with Grady just last night," her friend said. "You'd think he would have gotten the message."

"I suppose you were right about his intentions, but I'm more confused about what he's doing there. He knows I haven't been staying there, and he has my cell phone number. Why wouldn't he have called or texted?"

"I don't know. It is a little odd. Do you want me to go back to your house with you, just in case?"

Flora bit her lip and considered the offer. "Thanks, but I'm sure it's fine." She checked the live footage of her house. "It looks like he's gone now. I'll keep an eye on the security camera, but I don't think there will be any issues. I do need to stop by your place first, though. I need to get my overnight bag and my cat."

"I'll come with you," Violet said. "I'm glad you get to go home, but I'll miss having you around."

"I'll have a bonfire with everyone later this week," Flora promised. "Sydney's plan sounds like a good one. I'll text the group chat later to arrange it."

Back at the apartment, Violet helped Flora load her things into her truck before giving her a quick hug goodbye and then stepping back to wave as Flora pulled away from the curb. Flora raised her hand in the rearview mirror in one last wave before she focused on the road ahead of her.

She was beyond grateful to Violet for letting her stay at the apartment so unexpectedly and for so long, and made a mental note to figure out something nice to do for her friend. For now, though, she wanted to get back home and make sure everything there was okay.

When she turned onto her road and her house came into view, the first thing she noticed was that the plastic that had been covering the unfinished windows was gone, and the house looked great with its new, matching windows. She was glad she had gone with her gut and replaced them all, because it improved the way the house looked. It had been expensive, but on first glance the house would appeal to a lot more people now, and the new windows had the added benefit of offering better insulation, which was important both during the sweltering hot days of summer and the chilly winter.

The next thing she noticed was that the driveway was empty. She hadn't been able to check the security camera while she was driving, so the sight was a relief. Not that she was afraid of Linus. He was her friend… right? Or if not yet a friend, on his way to becoming one.

She parked her truck in its usual spot near the porch and unbuckled her seatbelt. Amaretto started meowing as soon she opened the door. She made sure her keys were ready, then grabbed the cat's carrier.

"Just give me two seconds," she told the cat as she carried her up the porch steps and unlocked the door. "Let me get your litter box set up, then I'll let you go. It's good to be home, isn't it?"

She left the meowing cat in her carrier in the living room while she brought her litter box and other supplies in from the truck. After getting the litter box set up in its usual spot, she opened the carrier's door so Amaretto could come out. The cat looked around cautiously, then relaxed. With a flick of her tail, she jumped onto the back of the couch and looked out the window, seeming happy to be back.

Flora went back outside to grab her overnight bag from the truck, and glanced over to Beth's house out of habit as she did so. Her eyes widened when she saw Sammy the Basset hound waddling down the road... alone.

She had no idea why the Yorks' dog was loose, but Beth would be heartbroken if he got hit by a car or lost. Flora ducked back inside to grab the bag of cat treats – she didn't think Sammy would mind that there was a cat instead of a dog on the front of the bag – then hurried out into the road, hoping no one would drive by until Sammy was safely back at Beth's house.

CHAPTER TWELVE

The dog quickened his pace when he saw her, his stubby little legs working their way up to a trot. She crouched down to look him over once she met him in the middle of the road. He looked up at her with his droopy eyes, his tail wagging slowly as she stroked his head.

"What are you doing out here, buddy?" she murmured. "You're not supposed to be wandering around like this, are you? Let's get you home."

She stood up and offered him a cat treat, then shook the bag and patted her leg as she started walking toward Beth's house. He followed her, happily wolfing down the occasional treat she fed him to keep his interest.

Flora's confusion over Sammy's presence on the

road without Beth turned into alarm as she neared her neighbor's house and saw that Beth's front door was open. She jogged the last few meters, tossed a few treats down on the porch to lure Sammy up, then knocked on the open door.

"Beth?" she called out. "Tim? It's Flora. I found Sammy wandering around outside. Is everything okay?"

There was no answer. After a moment, she pushed the door the rest of the way open and stepped inside. The interior of the house was silent except for the ticking of a clock. Sammy followed behind her, his claws ticking across the floor as he trotted into the kitchen, where he drank from his water bowl. The sound seemed loud in the otherwise quiet home.

There was no sign of Beth in the kitchen, so Flora continued into the living room. As soon as she stepped past the threshold, she froze. While the kitchen had looked normal, the living room was a mess. The drawers on the side table were open, the contents scattered everywhere. The jade statue Beth and Tim had gotten on their travels when they were younger was missing, as were the sterling silver plates Beth kept on a display against one of the walls.

Her worry beginning to take on a more urgent feel, she hurried through the house to Beth and Tim's bedroom. There, she found that the woman's jewelry box had been emptied, and on Tim's side of the room, the chest where he kept his old military awards was on its side, its contents strewn across the floor.

Someone had robbed the older couple blind, but even worse, both of them were missing. There was no sign of either Beth or Tim anywhere in the house.

She checked the back yard and the basement next, but they weren't anywhere to be found. Either they had been kidnapped, or they had gone somewhere else before their house was broken into. Maybe, just like with the break-in at her house, the thief had waited until he or she knew they were gone to act.

It wasn't the weekend yet, though, and that was when Beth's usual bus came. Flora tried to think of who else the older woman might get to give her and her husband a ride somewhere, and immediately landed on Natalie. The two of them had grown much closer since Natalie's husband passed away, and with Flora gone, Beth probably would have turned to her if she needed something.

She raced back outside, paused to make sure the front door was shut so Sammy couldn't get out again, then started jogging down the road toward Natalie's house, not wanting to waste the time it would take to go get her truck.

When she rounded the curve in the road, she was panting. Her physical labor on the house had made her stronger, but she hadn't done much in the way of cardio exercises, and now she was regretting it.

She slowed to a walk to try to catch her breath and frowned when she spotted Nolan's delivery van in Natalie's driveway. Natalie's car was gone, which supported her theory that the other woman had taken Beth and Tim somewhere.

Was Nolan here to deliver groceries to her? With Natalie gone, she would have expected him to leave them at the door, but his van was sitting empty, and there weren't any bags on the porch. As she got closer, she realized Natalie's door was partially open too.

Something was wrong here. With her breathing finally back under control, she eased her way up the porch steps silently and approached the door. She put her hand out to push it, and jerked back when someone kicked it the rest of the way open from inside. She came face-to-face with Nolan, who had a half-full black plastic trash bag in one hand. He froze, staring at her. She stared back.

Before either of them could say anything, she heard the sound of tires on gravel and turned to see a beat-up van pull into the driveway. It looked familiar, but it wasn't until she saw Duncan get out that she realized it was his and Tucker's work van. He looked around and seemed to note that Natalie's car was gone, if the crease between his eyebrows was any indication. When his eyes landed on Flora, he made his way toward the porch. Her feet seemed frozen in place, and Nolan didn't seem to know what to do either, because he didn't move.

"Look, I should have said this at the coffee shop, but I'm so sorry," he said to Flora. "Tucker told me what he was going to do. I told him he was being an idiot, and to leave me out of it, but I didn't stop him. He wasn't going to steal anything, he just wanted to poke around the house at night and have some fun. I hate that I didn't stop him. It's my fault that he's dead now."

"No, it isn't," Flora said. "No one could have known what was going to happen."

He took a deep, shaky breath. "Well, I'm here to pick up the last of our pay from Natalie. She told me she'd have it ready for me. Is she here?"

He had dark circles under his eyes and walked with a defeated slouch, but his eyes were sharp as they glanced between her and Nolan when both of them remained silent.

"What's going on?"

His gaze fell to the garbage bag in Nolan's hand. Nolan made to tuck it out of sight behind the wall, but the movement made it catch on the doorframe and it ripped open, sending a mess of jewelry, decorative figurines, and silverware clattering to the ground.

Nolan swore and dropped the bag, jumping back as if it had burned him. Flora's growing suspicion solidified itself, and she knew for a fact that he was the one who had ransacked Beth's house. She felt a sharp spike of anger.

"I can't believe you. Beth is one of the kindest women you'll ever meet, and you've been taking advantage of her. You've been using your visits to her house to figure out where they kept their valuables, haven't you?"

"No, wait, it's not what it looks like," he started, but Duncan spoke up before he could say anything else.

"This guy has been breaking into houses?" He glanced at Flora. "Is he the one who broke into *your* house?"

Nolan froze. Flora realized it all made sense. She took a step back, feeling sick.

"It *was* you," she breathed. "Beth told you I was going to be gone all night, and you would have seen the plastic covering the windows when you drove by.

You would have known it would be easy to get in and out without anyone seeing you. Only, Tucker was already there."

"I never meant to hurt anyone," Nolan said quickly, his voice laced with panic. "I should have been the only one there. When I heard Tucker sneaking in, I panicked. I thought it was you coming back." He glanced at Flora. "I thought I would be able to hit him with the lamp and get out of there while he was recovering, but it must've hit him wrong. He collapsed and I didn't realize until I heard the news in the morning that I had killed him.

"You killed my best friend," Duncan said. "I don't care if you didn't mean to. He's dead because of you!"

Duncan lunged at Nolan and the two fell to the ground, throwing punches and elbows. Flora jumped back, clapping her hands to her mouth. Nolan grabbed one of the larger figurines that had fallen to the ground when the garbage bag split open and raised it over his head, and Flora saw Duncan's eyes widen.

In the split second before it fell, she lunged forward and yanked the statue away from Nolan. He swore, though that was probably more because Duncan kicked him in the leg in the same moment.

Flora kept the figurine with her as she backed

away, trying to think of a way to make them stop fighting. The sound of someone else pulling into the driveway did it for her. The two men stopped their fight when Natalie's car door slammed shut. She froze when she saw the scene on her porch, her eyes flicking between the three of them coldly.

"I have no idea what's going on, but I'm not surprised to see you involved in it, Flora."

"Beth and Tim?" Flora asked desperately. "Are they okay? Nolan broke into their house, then he came here."

"They're fine. I took them to an appointment for Tim, and just dropped them off in front of their house. What's happening here?"

"He's the one who killed Tucker," Duncan panted as he scrambled to his feet, wiping at his bloody nose as he glared at Nolan.

Nolan looked between the three of them and seemed to realize he was outnumbered. He climbed to his feet as well, then began to back away into Natalie's house. A moment later, he turned and ran, and they all heard him slam the back door behind him as he exited from the other side of the house.

Natalie just stared after him, looking exhausted. Finally, she sighed and pulled out her phone.

"I'm calling the police," she said. "I hope the two

of you will stay to explain to them what happened. Then, Flora, I never want to see you on my property again."

Flora exchanged a look with Duncan, who looked a little chagrined. Things could have gone worse, she supposed. She just hoped the police caught up to Nolan before he could do any more harm.

EPILOGUE

Flora gave the paint roller one last push up the wall, then put it down and stepped back to gaze at the newly painted kitchen. Grady leaned against the counter next to her, his arms crossed as he admired it.

"It looks good," he said. "Are you going to get new counters too?"

"I'm not sure," she said. "These ones are dated, so I'd like to, but it's not a priority right now. I need to focus on getting things ready for Thanksgiving. My aunt is going to visit, and I think I'm going to invite the rest of my family too. I want the house to look nice for when they come, which means taking care of the most visible issues first."

"Let me know if you need any help. You know I'm always happy to pitch in."

She smiled. "I know. And I appreciate it more than you know. I wouldn't have been able to do all of this without you, Grady."

"Yes, you would have," he said. "You might have needed to watch a few more instructional videos than you would otherwise, but I know you could have figured it out."

She smiled, touched by his faith in her, and pressed a kiss to his cheek, glad that was something she could now do whenever she got the urge. A lot of the temporary awkwardness between them had faded, and she was glad of it. She knew she would have to talk to Linus at some point – the man had come to her house with flowers, for goodness sakes – but she thought he would understand. He had probably only shown up like that because he had been stood up by his date. For all she knew, those flowers had been intended for the woman who had stood him up, and he wanted to give them away rather than toss them in the trash.

It seemed the longer she lived in Warbler, the deeper and more complex her relationships got. Natalie wanted nothing to do with her, Beth was coming to rely on her for help when other services weren't available, she and Grady were dating, and

Violet was quickly becoming one of the best friends she had ever had.

Leaving was going to be difficult, but she didn't want to think of leaving right now. She leaned her shoulder against Grady's and sighed as she admired the kitchen. There was a lot to be happy about right now. She could worry about everything else later.

Printed in Great Britain
by Amazon

31323080R00063